Snow Bright and the Tooth Magician

BILL CONDON
Illustrated by Ian Forss

Published by
Sundance Publishing, LLC
33 Boston Post Road West
Suite 440
Marlborough, MA 01752
800-343-8204
www.sundancepub.com

Project commissioned and managed by
Lorraine Bambrough-Kelly, The Writer's Style
Designed by Cath Lindsey/design rescue

First published 1998 by
Addison Wesley Longman Australia Pty Limited
95 Coventry Street
South Melbourne 3205 Australia
Exclusive United States Distribution: Sundance Publishing

ISBN 978-0-7608-3286-8

Printed by Nordica International Ltd.
Manufactured in Guangzhou, China
May, 2010
Nordica Job#: 05-53-10
Sundance/Newbridge PO#: 225991

Contents

CHAPTER 1
Snow Bright, the Queen of Boppityboo 5

CHAPTER 2
The Magic Mirror Speaks! 9

CHAPTER 3
A Rotten Trick 13

CHAPTER 4
A Gummy Smile 17

CHAPTER 5
Mean Queen Irene 23

CHAPTER 6
Deadybones? 27

CHAPTER 7
Whizzbanger, the Tooth Magician 35

CHAPTER 8
Green Teeth and Shiny Bald 41

CHAPTER 9
The Smile Contest Begins 47

CHAPTER 10
The Shiniest Green Smile of All! 55

Dedicated to
Barbara Chapman and Dorothy Thorne

CHAPTER 1

Snow Bright, the Queen of Boppityboo

The kingdom of Boppityboo was famous all over the world for its annual Smile Contest. People trained every day of the year for the contest, looking into mirrors for hours on end and flashing their pearly-white teeth.

First prize in the contest was: two tons of toothpaste, two hundred toothbrushes, a race car, a speedboat, and a jet plane. AND the winner became the Queen of Boppityboo!

Snow Bright had won the Smile Contest for ten years in a row.

No one could beat her razzle-dazzle whopper of a smile. Every tooth in her mouth gleamed like the shiniest star.

Every year when she won, Snow Bright sold her prizes and gave the money to the poor people of the kingdom.

Snow Bright lived in the royal castle with her husband, the young and dashing Prince Charming. (His breath smelled a bit from eating lots of garlic pizzas, but otherwise he was great.)

Her best friends were seven champion sumo wrestlers—Frisky, Frosty, Floppy, Flippy, Fizzy, Fuzzy, and George.

Everything was perfect for Snow Bright, until . . .

CHAPTER 2

The Magic Mirror Speaks!

It was the day of the annual Smile Contest. Snow Bright had to win in order to remain queen. She'd won so many times before that no one expected her to lose.

But just to be sure, Snow Bright checked with the magic mirror.

Mirror, mirror, on the wall,
Who has the cutest smile of all?

Dark clouds swirled in the mirror. Slowly through the clouds appeared two tiny lights. The lights grew until Snow Bright saw that they were eyes. Then came a hairy nose and ears and a mouth—and finally the magic mirror said:

Oh, Snowie dear, I'm sad to say,
A better smiler's on the way.

Snow Bright scratched her chin. “And who might this better smiler be?”

The magic mirror’s voice shook in fear as it replied:

Her name is Irene.
She’s meaner than mean!

Snow Bright had never heard of anyone named Irene, but the sumos had.

"She's the sister of Jeannie, the former wicked Queen of Boppityboo," said Fuzzy.

"She is an even bigger crook than her sister. And she knows lots of rotten tricks." The sumos told Snow Bright all they knew about Irene.

Suddenly the mirror spoke again.

Take my tip and run away.
You'll be a dragon's dinner if you stay!

CHAPTER 3

A Rotten Trick

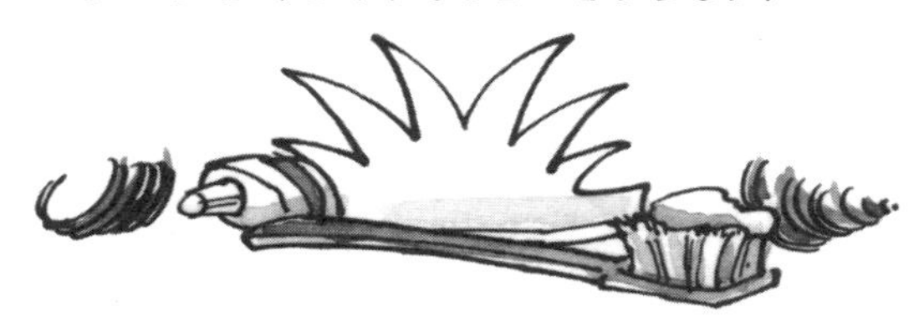

As they waited for the Smile Contest to begin, Prince Charming held Snow Bright's hand. "No one's going to hurt you while I'm around, my darling," he said.

The sumos stuck out their roly-poly tummies and burst into song.

Hi ho, hi ho,
We're mighty tough su-mo.
If someone tries to hurt Snow Bright,
We'll sit on them with all our might,
Hi ho, hi ho, hi ho!

A few moments later, the four Smile Contest judges entered the room. They wore their very best black suits and tall hats, and they never said a word.

"Let the Smile Contest begin!" declared Prince Charming.

Snow Bright was in a corner warming up her teeth, when a scruffy woman holding a tray of cookies burst out of the crowd.

"I have a present for you, Your Majesty," the woman said to Snow Bright. "I made these special cookies just for you."

"No, thanks. I'm not really hungry."

The poor woman sighed. “It took me so long to bake them, and I promise they’ll bring you luck in the Smile Contest.”

Snow Bright felt sorry for the woman and so, before anyone could stop her, she grabbed a cookie and took a huge bite.

“Ooh, ahh, oww!” she cried. “I think I’ve broken a tooth.”

She spit out a shiny tooth. Then another and another.

Her teeth flew out like shooting stars. In just a few seconds, she was totally toothless!

CHAPTER 4

A Gummy Smile

The poor woman whipped off her ragged cloak and shawl.

Underneath, she wore a beautiful red dress that was dotted with jewels.

"My name is Irene," she announced. "I'm here to win the Smile Contest."

"But you said your cookies would bring me luck," protested the toothless Snow Bright.

"Correct," snapped Irene. "Bad luck!"

Irene snarled at Snow Bright and her friends.

Then she turned to the judges and grinned like a hungry crocodile.

The judges held up their scorecards: 8.5, 9, 9.5, 9.9!

"You can beat that," said Prince Charming to his wife.

"Go for it, Snowie!" yelled the sumos.

Nervously, Snow Bright opened her mouth. She beamed a gummy smile at the judges.

Then, as the judges held up their scorecards that read 5, 6, 7, and 7.5, everyone frowned—except Irene.

Irene punched the air and skipped about with delight. "I won! I won!" she shouted.

Sadly, Snow Bright took off her golden crown and placed it on Irene's head.

"Congratulations," she said. "The best smile won. You are now Queen Irene of Boppityboo."

CHAPTER 5

Mean Queen Irene

The moment the crown was placed on her head, Queen Irene's smile turned into a nasty scowl.

A ripple of fear raced through the royal chamber.

Prince Charming and all the sumos gathered around Snow Bright.

“You’d better not hurt her,” said Fuzzy. “We’re sumo wrestlers, you know. Our stomachs are lethal weapons.”

“How dare you?” said Queen Irene. “I eat silly men like you for breakfast!”

Prince Charming rolled up his sleeves and flexed his muscles. "I'll bop the nose of anyone who touches my darling wife."

The new Queen of Boppityboo clapped her hands, and the royal guards came running.

Pointing at Prince Charming, she declared, "Take him to the dungeon. Lock him up and throw away the key."

Snow Bright fell to her knees. “Please don’t do that to my prince. The dungeon’s as cold as ice and full of mice.”

Prince Charming’s knees knocked. “Oh,” he shuddered, “mice aren’t nice.”

“Don’t worry,” said Queen Irene. “I’ll make sure you’re released—after a hundred years or so!”

CHAPTER 6

Deadybones?

The Queen waggled a finger at Snow Bright. "And you," she snarled, "will be fed to Rupert the Royal Dragon. Now!"

But, as the guards moved toward Snow Bright, the sumos pounced.

They bopped them with their bellies and bounced them with their bottoms.

In the next second, Snow Bright was on top of Frosty's shoulders. As fast as their little chubby legs could carry them, the sumos stormed out of the palace.

Queen Irene's eyes glowed like red-hot coals. She went bananas!

"I'll get you, Snow Bright!" she roared. "You and your horrid sumo friends will be deadybones!"

Snow Bright and the seven sumos didn't stop running for days.

At last they came to a tiny village where no one knew them.

There the sumos soon found work as sumo wrestling accountants. And every morning they left for work singing this song:

Hi ho, hi ho,
Accounting we will go.
It's too bad that we can't add,
Hi ho, hi ho, hi ho!

As soon as they were gone, Snow Bright left to find a dentist who could fix her teeth.

But every dentist in the village told her that she would have to get false teeth.

"No one can fix your real teeth," they said. "No one. Ever!"

CHAPTER 7

Whizzbanger, the Tooth Magician

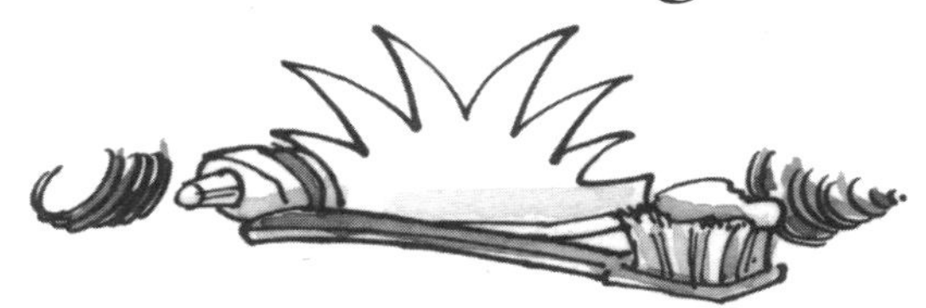

A year passed. Once again it was time for the Boppityboo Smile Contest. And still Snow Bright was toothless.

One day as she wandered through the streets, she saw a bright pink wagon. On its side was written:

Snow Bright rang the bell on the wagon door.

Instantly the door opened, and a round-faced man appeared.

"Hidey-ho and howdy-do," he said. "Whizzbanger's the name, and teeth are my game."

Snow Bright showed him her gummy mouth.

"I want my teeth back," she said, "but the dentists in the village say it's impossible."

Whizzbanger's eyes bulged. "I'm a tooth magician," he said proudly. "Nothing's impossible for me!"

Snow Bright opened her purse, but Whizzbanger shook his head. He wanted payment, of course, but he didn't want money.

"I'll give you beautiful teeth," he promised, "if you'll give me your gorgeous hair."

"I'm sure I could spare a bit of hair."

"No, no," Whizzbanger replied. "I want it all! I want to make a coat of beautiful hair."

Snow Bright hesitated for a moment, then agreed.

In a flash, an electric razor was in the tooth magician's hands. With a *whisssh* and a *whoooosh*, her hair was gone!

Snow Bright looked in the mirror, and her heart sank. Just as Whizzbanger had promised, her teeth had grown back. But instead of gleaming white teeth, she had a mouth full of gleaming *green* teeth!

"Sorry about that," said Whizzbanger. "I'm color-blind."

CHAPTER 8

Green Teeth and Shiny Bald

When the sumos returned home that evening, they got the shock of their lives.

"Aaarggghh!" they yelled, as they ran away.

Snow Bright, green-toothed and as bald as a bowling ball, quickly caught up with them and told her story.

“Don’t you see?” she said. “Now that I have my teeth back, I can enter the Smile Contest again. I’ll beat that mean Queen Irene and rescue Prince Charming!”

The sumos shook their heads and muttered among themselves. No one with green teeth had ever won the Smile Contest. And there had never been a bald queen in Boppityboo —or anywhere else, ever.

They knew they'd end up as dragon's dinner if they went to Boppityboo with Snow Bright, and she didn't win the contest.

But still they said, “Go for it, Snowie! We’re with you all the way!”

Snow Bright polished her hairless head until it shone almost as brightly as her green teeth.

To show their support, the seven sumos shaved off their hair, too.

Before long, Snow Bright and the sumos joined hands and headed off to the Smile Contest.

CHAPTER 9

The Smile Contest Begins

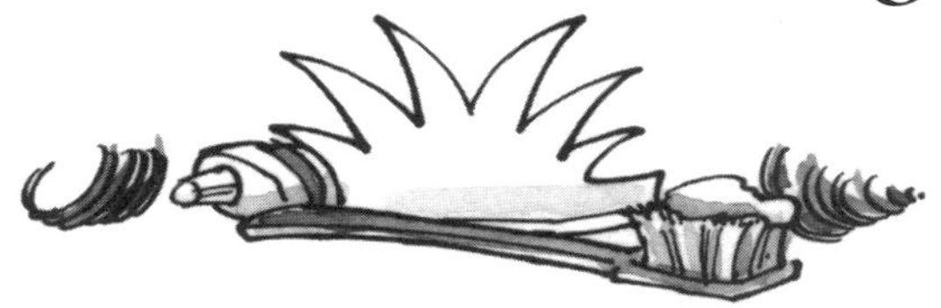

Queen Irene smiled confidently to herself. "No one can beat me in the Smile Contest," she said.

But just to be certain, she checked with the magic mirror.

Magic mirror on the wall,
Who has the shiniest smile of all?

Dark clouds swirled in the mirror. Slowly through the clouds appeared two tiny lights. The lights grew until Queen Irene saw that they were eyes. Then came a hairy nose and ears and a mouth—and finally the magic mirror said:

Oh, Queenie dear, I swear it's true,
No one's got a better smile than you.

Queen Irene giggled with delight, then raced off to the Smile Contest.

Up to the four contest judges she strode. "Let's get this over with," she said. "Here I am. Now declare me the winner."

Ͻne of the judges peeked over the Queen's
;houlder.

Γhe Queen turned around. How angry she
ɔecame when she saw Snow Bright and the
;umos!

However, as they drew closer, she began to laugh.

"You're all baldies!" she bellowed.

Then she saw Snow Bright's green teeth. She laughed so hard she almost fell over.

The sumos looked embarrassed, but not Snow Bright.

"Let the Smile Contest begin," Snow Bright told the judges.

CHAPTER 10

The Shiniest Green Smile of All!

Queen Irene shoved Snow Bright aside, licked her lips, and bared her gleaming teeth.

Without a word, the judges held up their scorecards: 8, 8.5, 9, 9.5.

"Yippee!" cried the Queen. "Try to beat that, you green-toothed baldie!"

The sumos crossed their fingers—*and* their toes.

Snow Bright fluttered her eyelashes and turned on her shiniest green smile.

Instantly the judges held up their scorecards: 10, 10, 10, 10.5.

"Snowie's won!" cried the sumos.

"Oh, so I did," she said. "What a lovely surprise!"

As Snow Bright and the sumos sang and danced, Queen Irene stomped over to the judges.

“Don’t you have eyes in your heads?” she shouted.

The judges didn’t answer.

"Look what you've done!" she growled. "You've given Boppityboo a green-toothed, bald-headed queen. What kind of judges are you?"

"Bald judges," they replied, as they took off their long, tall hats to reveal lots of shiny scalps—and not a single hair!

So that is how Snow Bright once again became Queen of Boppityboo.

The villagers tried to feed mean Irene to Rupert the Royal Dragon, but Rupert made a face and spit her out. She was never seen again.

Prince Charming was rescued from the dungeon, and he and Snow Bright lived happily ever after.

The seven sumos invented green toothpaste, and they lived happily ever after, too.

Now the people of Boppityboo all have green teeth. And every one of them is bald. If you go to the kingdom of Boppityboo today, you will probably hear this song:

Hi ho, hi ho,
Bald is beautiful, you know.
We have no hair, and we don't care,
Hi ho, hi ho, hi ho!

ABOUT THE AUTHOR

Bill Condon

Years ago, a dentist's suction hose accidentally slurped up Bill Condon's tongue. The tongue was returned in less than a month, but since then Bill has had a terrible fear of dentists. That's why he keeps his teeth hidden in a jelly jar in his refrigerator, where no dentist would ever think of looking—until now!

Bill lives on the coast of Australia, and has written more than 40 children's books. He enjoys making up silly stories about himself.

ABOUT THE ILLUSTRATOR

Ian Forss

It was during the Great Chalk Battle of '71 that Ian Forss received a direct hit from a flying eraser, and all his teeth were knocked out.

Not wanting to attract attention to himself, he quickly replaced them with a set of colored pencils from his pocket.

Since then, whenever he is given a good story to illustrate, he can't wait to sink his teeth right into it.